The Tuckshop Kid

PAT FLYNN grew up running around an old dairy farm in Queensland, before moving to the Australian Institute of Sport in Canberra on a tennis scholarship. After playing and coaching on the professional circuit he became a teacher, where his observations of young people—their interests and stories—led him to writing a book.

Now he writes books for a living, in a house near the beach on the Sunshine Coast. He likes to start the day off with a surf and end it walking along the beach with his wife and son.

His novel, *To the Light*, was shortlisted for the 2006 CBCA Awards in the Younger Readers category.

Other books by Pat Flynn

The Tuckshop Kid

Pat Flynn

Illustrated by Tom Jellett

PZ
7
.F7245
T83
2006

First published 2006 by University of Queensland Press
PO Box 6042, St Lucia, Queensland 4067 Australia

Reprinted 2007

www.uqp.uq.edu.au
www.patflynnwriter.com

Typeset by Peripheral Vision
Set in 11/15.25pt Rotis Semi Sans
Printed in Australia by McPherson's Printing Group

Queensland Government
Government
Arts Queensland

The Regional Arts Development Fund is a
Queensland Government and Council partnership
to support local arts and culture.

Cataloguing-in-Publication Data
National Library of Australia
Flynn, Pat, 1968- .
    The tuckshop kid.

    For middle to upper primary students.

    I. Jellett, Tom. II. Title.

A823.4

ISBN 978 0 7022 3567 2.

Chapter One

HOT FOOD

Meat Pie	$2.40
Potato Pie	$2.40
Mathematical Pie	$3.16
Hot Dog	$1.70
Cheese Dog	$1.90
Homework-Eating Dog	$2.00
Hamburger with Salad	$2.80
Hamburger without Salad	$2.60
Cheeseburger	$3.00
Cheeseburger without Cheese	$2.80
Chicken Nuggets	$0.40 each
Gold Nuggets (served in pan)	$40.00 each
Hot Chips	$1.50
Warmish Chips	$1.25
Chip off the Old Block	$1.00

Some kids star at sport, some are young Einsteins, some are born bullies and a couple make careers as class clowns. Some girls are pretty, some boys are tough, some can do backflips and some make you laugh. Some are poets and they know it. 'Every child has a special talent,' Mrs O'Neill, our school principal, always says, 'even if some of you don't know what it is yet.'

I'm lucky, I reckon, 'cause I know what I'm good at. It mightn't make me prime minister or an Olympic athlete or win me a prize on speech night, but at the beginning of lunch it's me that kids want to talk to. It's me they come to for advice.

Andy Reynolds jogs up as I enter the covered area. Around us kids run and scream, letting off some lunchtime steam. 'One ninety,' he says.

'Summin hot?' I say.

'Course.'

'Drink?'

'If possible.'

I don't even have to think, let alone look at a menu. The answer pops from my mouth like bubblegum. 'Two party pies and a plain milk. But if you ask nice you can get two squeezes of chocolate topping for nix. Shake it up and you got your very own milkshake.'

Andy squints, trying to remember what I'm saying.

'And I'd go to Jan 'cause Mrs Dwyer is mad at the world lately,' I add.

'Thanks, Matt. You're a legend!' He runs off.

'I know.'

Yep, I mightn't be the smartest, fastest or best looking, but I've got a special talent all right. It's called 'tuckshop'.

Trouble with giving other kids advice is that I don't have time to plan my own lunch, which is what I need to do right now. I'm leaning towards a meat pie (with sauce, of course) washed down by a slush puppy followed by a rainbow Billabong for dessert, but I'm not sure. Perhaps a cheeseburger, passiona and jelly cup? It's a tough decision. Tough but good.

There's no rush, because it's a good five minutes of waiting. Some kids, as soon as the teacher lets them out, run like the wind to make it to the front of the tuckshop line. When you've got a gut like mine, however, it's much easier to make wind than run like it. And to tell you the truth, I don't mind the waiting. The sense of anticipation, the smell of fried food, the smell of girls (let's face it, this is as close as I'm likely to get for a while) – it's all part of the tuckshop experience. Besides, what else am I gonna do during lunch break? Play 'chase the fat kid'? Not much fun when I'm the fat kid. After tuckshop I usually play handball, and 'cause I'm hopeless at handball I spend most of the game standing in line. I'd rather be in a line that smells like food than a line that smells like sweat.

Kayla slots in behind me, and butterflies zip around my tummy like pinballs. My tummy can fit a lot of butterflies so I'm full-on packing it. Kayla and I have this love/hate relationship. I love her and she hates me. No, that's not true. She's pretty nice to me sometimes. Though normally there's a reason.

She pokes me in the back. If anyone else did it I'd be annoyed, but from Kayla it feels like a massage. I turn around.

'What are you looking at, fatzilla?' says Tasha, the girl behind Kayla.

'Your ugly face,' I say. Tasha and I have a hate/hate relationship.

'You don't need tuckshop. You've got ten rolls under your shirt.' Tasha loves to have the last insult.

But so do I. 'At least I don't scare little kids just by looking at them.'

'Stop it, you two,' says Kayla. She looks at Tasha. 'I want to talk to my friend Matt for a second, okay?'

Tasha pokes her tongue at me.

Kayla puts an arm on my shoulder. I wish she'd take it off because I can't concentrate on what she's saying, and I know the only way to impress her is to give good advice.

'I haven't eaten all day,' she says. 'I'm *starving.*'

I know technically that's not true, but I don't disagree. 'How much you got?'

'See, that's the thing.' She paints on a smile that lights up her face and my insides. 'I really, really, *really* want a hamburger, but I've only got two dollars.'

'You can get a sausage roll and fifty cents worth of

4

lollies; I suggest.

She rolls her eyes.

'Three chicken nuggets and a Sunnyboy?'

She looks at me with puppy-dog eyes and gives my shoulder a squeeze. 'C'mon, Matt. Please? I'll be your best friend. Forever.'

One of the golden rules of the tuckshop line is never give in to scabs. Once you become known as a soft touch they'll come back again and again, like pigeons. I've had boys begging on their hands and knees, girls turning on fake tears like fountains, and not weakened.

Then Kayla came along. There are good scabs, there are pros, and there's Kayla. She uses touch, eye-contact, voice expression, promises – if scabbing was a subject, she'd get an A+ for sure.

As I give her 80 cents, our hands come together, if only for a second.

'I love you!' she says.

Even though I know she doesn't, hearing it makes me feel all warm inside, like hot chips.

Chapter Two

DRINKS

Flavoured Milk	$1.80
Plain Milk	$0.90
Low Fat Milk	$0.90
Plain Fat Milk	100 kilos
Poppers – apple, orange, tropical	$1.20
Nannas – blue hair, purple hair, no hair	$1.20
Soft Drinks – cola, lemon, orange	$1.30
Hard Drinks – iceberg, cement, algebra	$1.50
Sportswater	$2.00
Lazywater	$1.00
Slush Puppy	$2.00
Shoe-Eating Puppy	$2.00

Except for a few minutes at the start of lunch, I don't have many friends. I used to be best mates with Craig Withers until a new kid started calling him water buffalo. I told Craig to either ignore it or beat the hell out of the new kid, but for some reason it got to Withers – who's the second fattest kid in the school, behind yours truly. After that, Withers didn't want to be my mate anymore. In fact, he started teasing me more than anyone. And his new best friend? The new kid. When you're like me you learn something pretty quick. Life doesn't sense too much make.

But there is someone who's always nice to me: Jan the tuckshop lady. 'Well, if it isn't my young friend Matthew?' she says when I finally make it to the counter. 'What would you like today?'

Sometimes the other tuckshop lady, Mrs Dwyer, gives me a look as if to say, 'What are *you* doing here?' I like Jan heaps more than Mrs Dwyer, so I nearly always go in her line, even if it's longer.

'Hi, Jan.' I'm 80 cents poorer so a new lunch strategy must be quickly planned, but I thrive under pressure. 'Can I please have a cheese dog with sauce, barbeque chips and a plain milk?' I lean forward. 'And do you reckon I could have a couple of hits of chocolate topping in the milk?'

She smiles. 'Of course you could, darl, except there's no chocolate left. I just used up the last bit.' She gives me a wink. 'I think someone's been spreading our little secret.'

I look across the covered area to see Andy Reynolds shaking his milk up and down like a madman, spilling half of it.

Jan puts her mouth near my ear. 'How about I give you a chocolate one for the same price?'

Like I said, you gotta love Jan. Sometimes I have this dream that she's my mum, and in the dream we go on a picnic and there's a blanketful of beautiful food laid out on soft grass. And then Kayla comes up with melted chocolate over her fingers and puts them in my mouth and ... I think I've said too much already.

I take lunch to the handball courts. I'd prefer to sit at a table, but eating on my own would make me look like more of a loser than I already am, so I eat standing in the handball line. The cheese dog is superb. The roll is fresh but slightly toasted, so each bite has a soft crunch. The melted cheese melts in my mouth (as it should), and the dog is hot and tasty, especially with heaps of sauce over it. About ten blokes ask for a bite but I say no. I'm not getting scabbed on again this lunchtime.

With the chips and chocolate milk in my pockets, I get in then out of the dunce square in handball, which suits me fine because I want to finish my food. The chips disappear first, barbeque being tasty but causing a real thirst. It's impossible to drink while you eat at school, as it's a sure way to spill, drop or have something nicked. Rather than struggle with the crumbs, I give the chip packet away and open my milk. It's cold. It's chocolatey.

It's good.

Andy comes over. 'Why didn't you use the milkshake trick?'

'Someone used up all the chocolate.'

'Yeah, sure. You just wanna win a free one.'

'What do you mean?'

He points to the side of the milk carton. It says that one out of every ten chocolate milks is a winner. *Look inside when it's empty*, it says. I remind myself to do it.

I get into the game again and take an air-swing. Kids laugh and so do I.

Then someone yells from the stairs above: 'Good shot, pork chop!'

Kids laugh again, but I don't. On the stairs are Withers and the new kid.

'Watch out for the hippo behind you,' says Withers. 'Oh, that's right, it's your bum.'

He and the new kid high-five.

I imagine myself chasing and catching them, then sitting on their heads and breaking wind. But I'd be flat out catching a Year 1-er.

'Come here and say that,' I tempt them.

'I'd rather not get any closer to your man boobs,' says Withers.

'You've got a lot of guts, Withers.' I grab my stomach. 'A *lot* of guts.'

This makes everyone laugh but I don't feel too flash. In Year 2, when I was first teased about being fat, I'd get

11

real upset and find a teacher. They'd always say, 'Sticks and stones will break your bones but words will never hurt you.' What I want to say to teachers is this: you get called 'moo-cow' every day for a year and see how you feel. And because I know how it feels I'd rather not do it to Withers, except for one thing: he started it (which is something else teachers never seem to understand).

The bell rings and I finish my chocolate milk, and written on the bottom of the carton is a word which sums up how I never feel: 'WINNER!'

I walk quickly to the tuckshop and show Jan, who gives me a smile and a free drink. 'Put it in your bag for later,' she says.

'Okay.'

But when I get around the corner I skol it. It's just gonna go off in my bag, or get pinched, I reckon. And since that little confrontation with Withers I feel like a bit of a pick-me-up. But for some reason, this choccy milk doesn't taste as sweet as the first one. In fact, as I line up for class, I start to feel slightly sick in the stomach.

Chapter Three

FROZEN ITEMS

Fruit Juice Sticks	$0.50
Fruit Juice Stones	$0.50
Fruit Juice Bones	$0.50
Fruit Juice Words (will never hurt me)	$0.00
Sunny Boys	$0.70
Sunny Girls	$0.70
Cloudy Boys	$0.60
Cloudy Girls	$0.60
Icy Poles	$0.70
Icy Russians	$0.70
Icy U	$0.70
Uc Me	$0.70
Billabong – chocolate, rainbow, swagman	$1.00
Frozen Yoghurt	$1.30
Frozen Yoyo	(price goes up and down)

Mr Simpson stands at the front of class. He's tanned, muscly and fit.

This isn't good, I think. Our normal teacher, Mrs Spencer, is nowhere to be seen. Mr Simpson teaches Physical Education and we're supposed to have it on Thursday morning. I know this for a fact, because every Wednesday night I get Mum to write a note excusing me from PE.

'This week there's been a swap,' he says. 'As you know the cross-country race is coming up so we'll use this afternoon to get in some extra training.'

One boy actually says, 'Yes!'

A girl puts up her hand. 'I don't have my running shoes.'

Me either, I think.

'That's okay, you can run in bare feet.'

'Cool,' she says.

Not cool.

As I walk to the oval I have two thoughts:

1. *I don't have a note.*

2. *Why did I have that second chocolate milk?*

I decide to try and talk sense into Mr Simpson. Surely he doesn't expect *me* to run? I jog to catch up with him – even his walk is fast. 'Excuse me, sir.'

'Yes, Matthew?'

'I'm feeling sick, sir. I don't think I can run.'

'Do you have a note?'

'No, but –'

'If you don't have a note then you'll have to participate.' He looks at my stomach. 'Exercise is good for you, Matthew. Very good.'

This is bad, I think. *Very bad.*

'One lap to warm up,' Mr Simpson yells when we get to the oval.

As usual, I'm the last one back. And I'm a lot more than warm. I'm stuffed.

Kids are already stretching and Mr Simpson tells me to touch my toes.

'He can't even see his toes,' says Withers.

Lots of kids laugh and even Mr Simpson doesn't hide a smile.

'That's mean, sir,' Kayla says. 'You should tell Craig off for saying that.'

She gives me a little smile and I feel a little better, though the chocolate milk swishes around my stomach even faster.

'Everyone must run at least three laps,' orders Mr Simpson. 'Only then can you walk if you have to. Serious athletes should continue running until I blow the whistle.'

Kids line up like it's a race and Mr Simpson says 'Go'.

I run as slowly as I possibly can, but even so the two chocolate milks and cheese dog and chips all call up to me and say, 'This is a bad, bad idea.' It doesn't take long before I'm lapped, and some follow the lead of the new kid and slap me between the shoulder blades as they run past.

15

After the first lap I start walking, then Mr Simpson roars, 'Run, Matthew, or you'll do it tomorrow at lunchtime!'

I run. Halfway through the second lap I feel like I'm gonna barf. I try and take my mind off running and barfing and think of Kayla. Right then she jogs past and says, 'Keep going, Matt. You can do it!'

I start feeling better, and even run a bit faster. Then I hear Withers' voice from behind. 'Move over, boys. We're passing a wide load.'

Suddenly I start seeing spots, and then I see nothing at all. Nothing except blackness.

When I wake up, Mum is holding my hand. She looks stressed. This isn't unusual as Mum often looks stressed.

'Are you okay?' she asks.

'I don't know.'

'Do you have amnesia?'

'I can't remember.'

The school office lady comes in with an ice pack. She uses her happy voice. 'Feeling better are we? You just had a little faint, that's all. It's quite hot today.'

She puts the ice pack on my forehead. It's freezing.

A little faint? Like a nightmare things start coming back. 'Mr Simpson made me run,' I say to Mum.

'I'm sure it was just one of those things,' says the

office lady. 'Though you probably should visit a doctor just to check that everything's all right.'

Mum gives the office lady a death stare. She uses her quiet, angry voice. 'I *will* do that. And if the doctor tells me that I've been called out of a VERY important business meeting because of a teacher's incompetence, you can be assured I will be back to make a formal complaint.'

Go Mum!

I hop in the Beamer and realise that all the energy from fainting has made me peckish. 'Could we drive by Maccas?' I ask. 'I feel like a burger and fries.'

Mum gives me a death stare. I wish I hadn't asked.

'Do you know what it's like getting a phone call saying your child has collapsed?' she says.

Well, I don't have a child so ... no.

Mum answers her own question. Grown-ups do that a lot. 'It's scary, Matthew. Besides, I don't have time. I'm flat out at work at the moment.'

As if confirming what she said, Mum's car phone rings. It's Lincoln, her boss. His deep voice booms through the speakers. 'How's the boy?'

'He's okay,' Mum says.

'Good. Look, Lorraine, we're going to have to move quickly on the Steckworth account ...'

They start talking business and I start thinking of something else. Well, someone else. Even though it has been a bad day, Kayla said heaps of nice things to me,

17

although it's probably because I gave her 80 cents. Then again, maybe she likes me? Maybe she has a thing for big-boned blokes and I could be her very own teddy boy? Or maybe she doesn't care about looks, only about what I'm like on the inside. Which is sensitive, funny, smart ... Well, smart at tuckshop.

We pull up outside the doctor's surgery. Mum tells Lincoln she'll be back in an hour and checks her hair in the rear-view mirror. She smooths it over, covering the small bald spot she's got from pulling her hair out – strand by strand – when she's really stressed. She doesn't think I notice this, but I do.

As I walk into the waiting room, I see a girl who looks a bit like Kayla and I smile at her, hoping for one in return. If Kayla likes me, maybe this girl will too?

She scrunches up her nose and turns away.

Who am I kidding? I think. No one likes the fat kid.

Chapter Four

LOLLIES

Jellybeans	$0.70
Jellypeas (green only)	$0.70
Jellybelly	$0.70
Redskin	$0.60
Blistered Skin	$0.60
Peeling Skin (served in bite-sized chunks)	$0.60
Mixed Lollies	$0.50
Anti-social Lollies	$0.50
Lollipop	$0.40
Lollipop	$0.40
Oh Lolly, Lollipop ♫♫♫♫	$0.40
Frogs - red, green, bull	$0.30

'Doctor Morrison will see you now,' the receptionist says in a hushed tone.

Mum and I walk into a small room packed with medical stuff. On a shelf is a jar with a blue eye inside, floating. I take a gulp. My eyes are blue.

The doctor shakes my hand. 'How are you, Matthew?'

Great! I think. *That's why I'm seeing a doctor.*

'He collapsed during PE,' Mum says.

'Mmm. What were you doing?' the doctor asks me.

'Running,' says Mum. 'Fancy making kids run in this heat?'

'Mmm. How far did you run, Matthew?'

Mum doesn't know the answer to that question.

'Umm. About two laps,' I say.

'Were you sprinting?'

Even though I don't remember it too well, I know the answer. 'No.' I never sprint.

'Well, let's have a look at you, shall we?'

Why do adults say 'we' when they really mean 'me'? Or in Doctor Morrison's case, him and his cold, metal equipment. After I take off my shirt and shoes he listens to my heartbeat, hits me on the knee with a drumstick (I wish it was fried chicken), takes a prick of my blood, and then full-on tortures me – making me stand on a weighing machine.

After the tests I get dressed. Doctor Morrison looks at Mum, then at me. 'I don't like to say this, but you're not a well boy, Matthew.'

21

Mum looks stressed.

The doctor continues: 'I'll have to do some urine tests ...'

I try not to giggle. He said 'urine'.

'... but I think you may have type 2 diabetes. I don't want to scare you, but it's a disease with serious complications – including possible blindness and limb amputation.'

He mightn't *like* to scare me but he's good at it. I blink and touch my arm.

Mum looks even more stressed. 'What sort of treatment will he need? Insulin injections? Tablets?'

'Perhaps. But first Matthew needs to lose weight, become more active, and eat healthy, balanced meals.'

What? My idea of a balanced meal is a pie in one hand and a coke in the other.

Mum's quiet for a moment. This usually means her can-do, business brain is ticking away. 'I have a client who had his stomach stapled. He lost 40 kilos in six months –'

'Impossible,' says the doctor. 'Matthew's far too young.'

For once I agree with the doc.

Mum has another thought. 'I could order Slim Fit meals. They deliver healthy, ready-to-eat dinners for $200 a week.'

'Again, not really appropriate for a boy Matthew's age.'

No, definitely not. Healthy always means yucky.

'It's just that, well, I'm very busy with work, Doctor. I don't have time to cook. Actually, I can't cook. I know Matthew's big for his age but he's a good kid. Never gives me any trouble. I bring home dinner at night, give him money for lunch. He doesn't eat that much, he's just naturally large.'

The doctor turns to me. 'What did you have for dinner last night, Matthew?'

I remember it well. 'Pizza. Meatlovers with barbeque sauce.' The thought of it makes me hungry. 'Can we have it again tonight, Mum?'

She doesn't answer.

'And for lunch today?' asks the doctor.

'A cheese dog, barbeque chips and a chocolate milk. Well, two chocolate milks – I won a free one.' I smile at Mum but she doesn't smile back.

Instead, she takes out her mobile. 'Lincoln? Yeah, it's me. I won't be back at work today. My son needs some attention.'

I don't like the sound of this. Not at all. You see, Mum and I have an understanding. She lives to work, I live to have fun. As long as I get tuckshop money, a top-of-the-line TV/DVD entertainment system and my own computer, I don't bother her. I don't make her feel guilty for getting home so wound up from trying to please rich, fussy clients that the last thing she needs to deal with is a kid. I leave her alone and she pretty much leaves me alone, but it looks like that's all about to change. I think

24

I've just become her latest client.

We're there for ages. The doc writes out all the food I'm allowed to eat, and how much, and even gives Mum a cooking lesson. He talks about exercise – suggesting walking and playing games rather than cross-country running. Then he asks to speak to me on my own. I'm having a hard time concentrating because on his desk is a jar of jellybeans. I really feel like one. Preferably red, but I'd take any colour, even black.

'You know, people eat for a lot of different reasons,' the doc says. 'Sometimes because they don't feel so good about themselves. Why do you think you like to eat?'

I think for a second. 'Because it tastes good.'

He smiles. 'I want you to try something for me, okay?'

I don't nod. I want to see what it is first. Then again, nodding might help me get a jellybean.

'I want you to like the Matthew you are right now, while at the same time looking forward to the new, healthy Matthew you're going to become. Understand?'

I don't, but I nod anyway. I'm still thinking about the jellybeans. Maybe I'll get a handful?

He shakes my hand. 'Your Mum's right, Matthew, you're a good kid. I'll see you in a week, okay?'

Damn! No jellybeans.

Chapter Five

SANDWICHES

Vegemite, Promite, Marmite, G'daymate	$1.00
Banana	$1.20
Cheese	$1.50
Tomato	$1.50
Banana, Cheese and Tomato	$1.80
Egg	$1.70
Chicken	$2.20
Chicken	$2.20
Egg (which comes first, chicken or egg?)	$1.70
Curried Egg (looks like spew)	$1.80
Salad (tastes like spew)	$2.00
Tuna	$2.10
Ham	$2.00
All other available animals except Rat	$1.90
Rat	$2.00

Extras

Cheese	.50	Sauce	.20
Carrot	.40	Mayonnaise	.20
Cucumber	.40	Tomato	.40
Lettuce	.40	Hair	.20
Insect (alive)	.10	Insect (dead)	.05
Goober	.05	Booger	.05

26

On the way home we shop, and for the first time ever Mum heads straight for the fruit section. We pass the junk food aisle without rolling down and grabbing some treats. It's agony. If there weren't security cameras, I reckon I'd stash a family block of rocky road chocolate down my jocks.

At home, Mum actually cooks. It's not pretty. She throws all this yucky stuff starting with 'v' into a pot. I forget what it's called. Oh, that's right, vegetables. She gets out a small bit of fish and forgets to deep-fry it. Even worse, she forgets the chips.

For dessert we have fruit-salad. No ice-cream, no chocolate topping, no good stuff. I don't think my body can handle such a drastic change. It wouldn't surprise me if, in my sleep tonight, I walk to the kitchen and stuff spoonfuls of Milo into my gob. Actually, maybe I can set my alarm and *pretend* I'm sleepwalking. If I get caught, that is.

Later, Mum comes into my room and sits on my bed. Normally she says goodnight and goes to her laptop with a bottle of wind-down. Tonight she strokes my hair, and stays so long I pretend to be asleep, just so she'll realise it's okay to leave.

She whispers, like she doesn't want me to hear. 'After your dad left, I wanted so much to feel like a success. So I worked and worked, and now I earn lots of money and order twenty people around. And you know what? I feel like more of a failure than ever.'

27

She kisses me and I feel warm wetness against my cheek. I realise later it's my mum's tears.

As I drift off to sleep I hear a scary noise. It's the rumbling of my own belly.

'Can I have a ham and salad sandwich with …'

It hurts me to say this next bit.

'… no butter, please, Jan. Also, an apple and a chocolate milk, thanks.'

Actually, it hurts me to say all of it, except for the chocolate milk. I fully intended to order a pork riblet roll, a lamington and a packet of chips, but after Mum's performance last night I've got a strange feeling swirling around my insides. I think it's called guilt.

'Eating healthy, are we?' says Jan. 'Well, good for you.' She gives me an even bigger smile than usual.

I go and play handball. Well, line up to play handball. While we wait, Andy Reynolds fills in the gaps of yesterday. 'You went out like a light, dude. We all thought you were dead. Then we thought Mr Simpson was going to do mouth-to-mouth on you.'

'Gross,' I say.

'The funniest thing, though …' Andy is laughing already. '… Mr Simpson made Withers and the new kid help him carry you to the office. When they picked up your legs, you ripped one out, right in their faces.'

'But I was unconscious.'

'That's what's so cool about it!'

I laugh as well.

It's nearly my turn to play when Withers, the new kid, and a couple of other blokes who reckon they're more popular than they really are, come over. 'Hey, tubby,' says the new kid. 'Wanna go for a run?'

'Why don't you go back to your old school?' I say. 'Juvenile detention.'

'You were like a beached whale yesterday,' says Withers. 'Except a whale doesn't have so much blubber.'

'Like you're not fat too,' I say. 'At least I'm not in denial.'

'At least I'm not in a fatsuit.'

Kids laugh.

I get in the game and the ball is served to me, but I don't hit it. Instead, I catch it, turn and throw it square at Withers' head. Even though I'm usually as coordinated as a giant baby, somehow it smacks him flush on the left eye (although he's facing me, so it must be his right eye).

He stands there for a second in disbelief, and so do I. When you try something like this, you don't expect it to work. Then Craig falls to his knees, puts two hands over his face and starts howling like a run-over rabbit. He always was a wimp.

I walk off.

Under a tree I wait for trouble to find me, chuck the apple into a bush and enjoy my chocolate milk. Before

long someone pokes me in the back.

'Whaccha doing?' asks Kayla.

'Nuthin.'

'I heard what you did to Craig. The teachers are looking for you.'

I nod. I'm expecting it.

'I reckon he deserved it,' she says. 'He's so mean to you.'

I shrug.

'What happened yesterday? Are you all right and that?'

'Yeah. Well, sort of. They think I've got diabetes.'

Her eyes go big. 'You're gonna die of ... beatties! What's beatties?'

'No. Diabetes. It's this disease that ... fat people get.'

'How do you get rid of it?'

'Eat nothing but air and run a marathon every day.'

'Really?'

I give a little smile.

She pokes me in the shoulder.

I suddenly get suspicious. 'Why are you talking to me?'

'What do you mean?'

'Like, do you want something?'

'Do I need a reason to talk to a nice guy like you?'

Striding across the school is a teacher and a posse of kids, and one boy's pointing in my direction. But it's weird, because although I'm about to get busted big-time, I'm not as upset as I should be. Kayla just called me a nice guy.

'Have you finished your chocolate milk?' asks Kayla.

'What?'

'Give me your carton. I'll put it in the bin for you.'

My heart sinks. Now I know why she sat next to me, why she was being so nice. I don't know why I let myself believe things that aren't true. Before I hand it to her, I sneak a look at the bottom of the carton, and it's like looking at the bottom of my soul. Except the bottom of the carton calls me a WINNER!, and I reckon the bottom of my soul has a giant L tattooed on it.

'There he is!' says a boy. 'The fat kid who went psycho!'

'Matthew, Matthew, Matthew,' says the teacher. 'Mrs O'Neill is waiting to see you.'

'Have a nice drink,' I say to Kayla, before I'm led away.

Chapter Six

CAKES

Fruit Cake	$1.00
Insane Cake	$-1.00
Muffins Choc Chip (large)	$1.80
Muffins Choc Chip (small)	$1.00
Muffins Micro Chip (very, very small)	$1000.00
Lamington	$0.90
Sheepington	$0.90
Mud Cake	$1.30
Mud Pie (ingredients fresh from school creek)	$1.30
Poppyseed (a lot of things in the old days ...)	50 years ago
Apricot Tart	$1.10
Custard Tart	$1.10
Busted Heart	$1.00

Mrs O'Neill is shorter than many of the students. She speaks soft and slow, leaving the yelling to our deputy, Mr Brown. His thunderous voice can scare the pants off kids (or scare something wet into their pants). So you might think that a talk with Mrs O'Neill in her air-conditioned office isn't so bad.

You'd be wrong.

'Sit down, Matthew.'

She leans back and holds her chin in three fingers, not saying anything for a long time, and looks at me. Just looks. Though not at my flabby arms or my messy hair or even the one freckle on my nose, but at my eyes. Right *into* my eyes. And for some reason I find it impossible to look away. It's like her stare is a bright light and I'm a kangaroo about to get bowled over, or shot. I realise she's giving me the infamous 'O'Neill look', the one that Andy Reynolds reckons can make the toughest boy cry. I haven't cried in months so I'm quietly confident I can stave off tears, but know I'm in deep doo-doo.

'Tell me what happened,' she says, finally.

Now a lot of things have happened to me lately. I've fainted, been to the doctor, eaten a sandwich without butter. But I suppose I know what she's talking about.

'I was playing handball,' I say slowly, 'with some of the boys. There were other boys watching. Someone served me the ball. I think it was Andy Reynolds or Joe Haase. Or it could've been David Garrett, I dunno . . .'

Why aren't I fainting? Stupid, good-for-nothing diabetes.

'Anyway, I hit this really hard shot and it came off the side of my hand ...'

Side of my hand? Where'd you pull that one from?

'... and it accidentally hit Craig Withers in the eye. Accidentally.'

She doesn't say anything, just gives me another 'O'Neill look'. I start feeling like I would if one of my pets died, although I don't own any pets.

Eventually, she speaks. 'I'm disappointed in you, Matthew. Very, very, very disappointed.'

Please. Whatever happens, don't cry!

'I would've thought you'd be able to tell me the truth.'

More silence, another 'O'Neill look', and tears start to show up like unwanted relatives.

'Now, tell me again. What happened?'

'I threw the ball at Craig,' I blubber.

I reckon I've reached a new low, turning into a wuss in less than five minutes. I'm worse than Withers.

'Why?' she asks.

'Because. Just ... because.'

'Did he say something to you?'

I don't answer.

Last year I made a decision to stop telling teachers when I got teased. It's not like it never helped – sometimes it did. The comments would stop for a while, and the worst kids would act all nice to me in front of the teachers, trying to suck up. But I realised there's only so much teachers can do. I don't want kids to act nice to me because they have to. I don't want to be no charity case. And I don't want Kayla to think I'm a bloke who can't handle his own problems.

'Craig said you were mad at him because he doesn't want to be your friend anymore,' Mrs O'Neill says. 'Is that true?'

No! I think. But I don't say anything.

She sighs. 'Like I said, I'm disappointed. Just because you're bigger than other kids doesn't mean you can hurt them. Violence is not acceptable in our school. Do you understand?'

I nod.

She continues: 'I should suspend you, you know that. But because you've never done anything like this before I'm going to let you off with a week of detentions.'

'Thanks, Mrs O'Neill.'

I can't believe I've just thanked someone for giving me detention. I get up to leave.

'And Matthew.'

I turn around.

'Next time tell the truth. If you don't, you're only lying to yourself.'

That afternoon I open the front door to my house and get a huge scare. Mum's home.

'What are you doing here?' I ask.

She kisses me on the forehead. 'Just wanted to spend some quality time with my son.'

After a day like today, the last thing I feel like is quality time with my mother. I'd rather veg out in front of the tube.

'How was school?' she asks.

I start getting suspicious. Perhaps Mrs O'Neill called her at work?

'It was ... okay. How was work?'

She bites her lip. 'Okay.'

'Good.'

'Good.'

There's a pause.

'I baked you a cake for afternoon tea,' she says. 'A fruit cake. It's supposed to be both healthy and delicious.'

I have a small bite. It'd better be healthy because it's certainly not delicious. In fact, I reckon it's the worst thing I've tasted that hasn't been able to run away after I've bitten it. 'Mum, this is shockin'.'

She gives a little smile. 'I know.'

We walk to the park and chuck the Frisbee around. I don't think we've done this since the X-Box was invented. One slips through Mum's fingers and hits her right in the noggin. Falcon. It doesn't hurt her, though, 'cause she's got a hard head. I go for a between-the-legs grab and catch one in the groin. It kills.

Apart from minor injuries, the afternoon is a lot more

fun than I thought it would be – although I hope no kids from school see me playing Frisbee with my mum. Afterwards, we take the cake out of the car and feed it to the birds. Well, bird. There's only one around. It takes a peck, squawks, and flies off like it's running late to migrate.

Mum and I look at each other, and laugh like we've never laughed before.

Chapter Seven

HOW TO ORDER

PAPER BAGS MUST BE USED (not plastic) and
marked with your NAME, YEAR LEVEL and HOW MUCH
MONEY is enclosed. A separate bag for DRINKS
is preferred, marked in the same fashion as the
lunch bag. Any CHANGE will be TAPED to the
OUTSIDE OF THE BAG. CAPITALS ARE USED FOR
IMPORTANT INFORMATION BECAUSE SEVEN OUT OF TEN
PEOPLE ONLY READ IMPORTANT INFORMATION. Here is
a test to see if you are one of those people:

YOU ARE A GREAT big, crazy PERSON and I LOVE
messin' with YOU!

Detention means that I have to order my lunch, as I don't have time to line up for tuckshop and make it to the detention room before 1 pm. I hate ordering, because it means I have to decide in the morning, and no one really knows what they feel like for lunch until lunchtime. It's like trying to guess the future.

As I'm writing on the bag, Marcus Wright comes over. Marcus is like some world champion tennis player for his age, and all the girls love him because he's going to be rich and famous for hitting a fluffy, yellow ball over a net. (Big deal.) He's also a nice bloke, but why wouldn't you be if you're going to be rich and famous and all the girls love you?

'Hey, Matt,' he says.

'Hey, Marcus.'

'I was wondering if you could do me a favour?'

I tend to lose concentration when popular kids talk to me. My brain seems to have a mind of its own. *What can I do for you?* I think. *Teach you how to hit a tennis ball into your opponent's eye?*

Marcus says, 'Kayla told me ...'

Stay away from her, you underhanded player! The score between you two will never be love!

'... that you always win free chocolate milks. She said you're gifted or something. My dietician says I need a double dose of calcium before my three-hour training session after school, so if I give you money would you be able to order me a carton for lunch?'

41

The request catches me by surprise. Because it has led to some bad experiences, I wasn't planning on buying a chocolate milk today.

'Sure,' I say. 'But I can't promise it'll win.'

'Kayla says it will.'

I shrug.

At lunch I pick up my bagful of food – a cheese and salad sandwich, a small tub of fruit salad and a chocolate milk. The chocolate milk is the only half-decent thing in there, and it occurs to me that I really want it. I've got twenty minutes of looking up words in the dictionary and copying down their meanings to look forward to, so something sweet to drink would go down a treat. But before I get a chance to skol and tell Marcus I forgot, he shows up.

'Thanks, Matt.'

He rips the carton open and drinks it in two tilts of the head, and although I can do it in one it's still an impressive performance. He peers into the container and gets mad. 'Matt! I thought you always won!'

'I didn't promise anything.'

He steps in front of me and I get ready to defend myself in case he tries a forehand volley to the gut or a backhand smash to the kidney. Instead, he shows me the carton, and I'm confused because it says 'WINNER!'

Marcus smiles. 'I was just pulling ya leg, mate. You aced it! You're in the zone!'

In the zone? Cool.

I look at my watch. I may be in the zone but I'm supposed to be in detention.

'Fallacious', 'antilogous' and 'subreptitious' all mean 'illogical'. In other words, something doesn't add up, it's bogus, there's like no possible way, man. After four days of detentions I know such words. I also know that winning free chocolate milks five lunchtimes in a row is fallacious, antilogous *and* subreptitious, but that's what has happened. When it comes to winning chocolate milks, I'm still in the zone.

After he won, Marcus told Jasmine – the second prettiest girl in our school (behind Kayla) – and she had me win a free one for her and her best friend, Nina. When I got out of detention, Jasmine and Nina were waiting and they both gave me a hug. (I was actually scared to squeeze in case I snapped them in half. They're about size 2.)

Then Eric, the toughest kid in our grade, heard about it, and you don't say no to Eric. When he won, he said I could have one favour, kind of like the Tim Tam genie. Except Eric is more of a mafia genie. I thought about having him beat up Withers and the new kid, but instead I asked him to punch me in the gut if he ever saw me eating fried food. He said it'd be his pleasure.

Somehow Mrs Spencer caught wind of my luck

(better than catching wind of my wind), and today she offers me a deal. If I can win a free chocolate milk for her son (that's what she says – she probably wants it for herself) she'll pull some strings and get me out of the fifth and final detention tomorrow. She gives me the money, I hand over the milk, and she sucks it through a straw while we do a maths worksheet after lunch. The whole class is quiet, waiting to see whether or not she wins. I think most hope she will, but seeing a teacher lose and me get another detention is an attractive prospect to some kids. When it's empty, she takes the carton outside to wash it, leaving me in charge. 'If any students misbehave while I'm gone, Matt, write their names on the board and they will join you in detention tomorrow. Well, if you *are* in detention, that is.'

Some kids are silly but I can't be bothered scribbling down their names. The last thing a chubby kid needs is more enemies.

When Mrs Spencer comes back, kids are eager to know how she went. 'Did ya win, Miss? Did ya, did ya? Did ya win?'

'When you're quiet I'll tell you.'

You can hear a pen drop.

She gives me a serious look. 'I'm afraid, Matthew, that tomorrow at lunchtime you have ... no detention. I won!'

The class cheers and a few kids rush over and slap me on the back. It stings, especially when Eric does it.

'Okay, that's enough,' says Mrs Spencer. 'Sit down now.'

Kids don't, of course, and in the commotion Kayla lobs a folded-up piece of paper onto my desk.

'Hurry up!' says Mrs Spencer, louder.

As the class settles down, I unfold the note.

Dear Matt
You're the best!
Love Kayla
xxxOOO

When I look over she gives me a huge smile. I feel like I've just died and ate a Heaven.

Chapter Eight

FRUIT AND SALADS

Apple, Banana, Orange, Pear	$0.70
Special - pair of pears	$1.00
Fruit Salad - small	$2.00
Fruit Salad - large	$3.00
Fruit Salad - ginormous	
(served in swimming pool)	$100.00
Garden Salad	$2.20
Garden Salad with Chicken, Ham, Tuna,	
or Roses	$3.00
Tossed Salad	$2.50
Tossed Salad with Duck!	$2.50
Boiled Egg - Hard	$0.60
Boiled Egg - Runny	$0.60
Boiled Egg - Walky	$0.60
Boiled Egg - Talky	$0.60
Moderately Warm Egg	$0.50

Pat Flynn

Something else is fallacious, antilogous and subreptitious in my life. Mum's home early every afternoon this week.

'Do you even work anymore?' I ask.

'Yeah,' she says with a smile. 'But I've told Lincoln I want fewer hours.'

'Really? What did he say?'

Lincoln is the only person in the world who works harder than my mum. If there was a workaholic's anonymous meeting, he'd be the first to show up and the last to leave.

'He grumbled and mumbled, but I make him a lot of money so what can he do? There's a new whiz-kid who knows everything about everything. He's taken over half of my accounts, and if it works out I'll be home most afternoons.'

It takes a few seconds for this to sink in. 'Are you going to be all right?'

She looks at me, a hint of worry on her face. 'What do you mean?'

'You know. Are you going to be okay . . . not working all the time?' Mum without work is like a cheeseburger without cheese.

She runs a hand through my hair. 'I think so. We both know I'm happier when I'm busy, but here I can cook, exercise with you and help with your homework.'

I can't think of anything worse than exercising, doing homework and eating my mum's cooking. Then all of a sudden I can. 'How about money?' I ask. 'Will you make heaps less?'

What I mean is, will you still make enough to buy me the latest DVDs and computer games?

'I will make less,' she says, 'but I think it'll be worth it, don't you?'

I'm not sure about this so I don't answer.

'Besides,' she adds, 'I don't think we'll starve.'

Talking about starving, I realise I'd love a bit of afternoon tea. I rub my stomach and Mum reads my mind.

She opens the fridge and pulls out an ice-cream container. I get excited until I realise there's no ice-cream in it.

'Apricot slice,' Mum says. 'I found the recipe on the Internet. No butter and hardly any sugar.'

Oh no!

She gives me a piece. It's not the best but I have to admit it's a lot tastier than the fruit cake.

'You've got a lot better,' I say, surprised.

'Oh, thanks.'

'I mean it, Mum. It's almost edible.'

Suddenly, she turns away, and I bend around so I can see her face. There's a tiny waterfall trickling down her cheek.

'I was only joking,' I say quickly. 'Look.' I take another bite.

'It's not that.' She wipes her eye with the inside of her

wrist. 'It's just . . . I wish I could be a better mother, that's all.'

'You're heaps good. You buy me cool stuff and . . .'

I hate it when I say 'and' and then can't think of anything to say after it.

'Anyway,' I add, 'I bet you didn't think you'd end up with a son like me.'

For some reason, this doesn't make her feel better. The waterfall starts again, more of a stream this time than a trickle.

'Don't you ever think that,' she says, taking me in her arms. 'I'm lucky to have you.'

She looks into my eyes. 'I love you so much. It's just that . . . I don't always love me.'

All Mum's tears are starting to make me a bit sad. I bury my head in her shoulder. 'Well, *I* love you,' I say.

But I don't think she hears.

Although I've won my way out of detention, Thursday has something even worse. PE.

'Hurry up, people. The grass won't bite. At least three times around without walking,' says Mr Simpson.

I reckon he shouldn't call it cross-country training. Round-oval training is more accurate.

He claps his hands. 'C'mon, people. Get moving. Except Matthew. You come over here.'

I wonder what's going on. He's probably going to give me one of his boring pep-talks.

'You can sit under a tree and watch,' he says. 'I don't want a repeat of last week.'

Now normally I'm happy as a pig in mud to sit in the shade during PE, but today something inside me snaps. 'I'd rather not, if that's okay.'

'What?'

What? I'm not sure why I said it. Perhaps because every Thursday Mr Simpson reads my mum's note and says, 'Matthew, Matthew. When are you going to learn that exercise is good?' Today he hasn't even asked for the note (although it's in my back pocket). It's like he's given up on me.

'I'd rather run,' I say.

'Why?'

'Because, sir, when are you going to learn that exercise is good?'

I run off.

After two laps I wonder how I could've been so stupid. I'd succumbed to a rare moment of weakness – for the first time in my life I cared about being the most unfit person on the face of the planet. That sort of attitude will get me into a lot of trouble if I'm not careful.

Sweat starts to drip into every crack of my body, and it's not good. I think about taking a detour to the shady tree.

Kayla catches up to me. (Actually, she's lapping me.) She jogs beside me for a bit. 'Wow, Matthew. You're doing great!'

I am? I remember that every afternoon this week I've done some form of exercise. Mum and I rescued dusty bikes from the back of the shed and rode to the park. We drove to a dam, hired a canoe and rowed for twenty minutes before capsizing. (Okay, I did it on purpose.) And most tiring of all, we walked around a massive shopping centre for an hour. *Perhaps I can do this?*

Kayla interrupts my train of thought. 'I want to talk to you about something later, okay?'

I try to say 'Yes' but no word comes out. I'm breathing too hard. Instead, I nod.

Withers and the new kid run past. They slow down to deliver an insult. 'Hey, there's Kayla and her new boyfriend,' says Withers. 'The Goodyear blimp.'

If I had any energy I'd tell him to duck next time someone threw a tennis ball at his face. But I don't, so I don't.

Kayla also doesn't spit out a comeback line. Her face is red, but I'm hoping it's just from the running. She speeds up and passes the boys. When she does, I notice how hard Withers is breathing – almost as hard as I am. And I'm breathing heavily enough to blow out the birthday candles of someone turning 100.

When I've done two and a half laps Mr Simpson blows his whistle. Most kids have done four or five laps, the real good runners more than six. Kids cut across the oval to the finish line, but in another rare moment of weakness, I don't. For some reason I feel like I've got a point to prove, so I keep plodding along, one step at a time.

Something strange starts happening. Instead of talking to Mr Simpson or each other, kids look at me. A group starts to crowd around the finish line.

'Yeah, Matt!' yells Jasmine. 'Keep going!'

What do you think I'm going to do? Turn around?

'You the man!' screams Andy.

Now I'd love to sprint home and be a hero. The trouble is that by this stage I'm completely knackered. I'm also starting to feel a bit sick in the gut (though at least there's no chocolate milk swishing around in there) and possibly a touch dizzy, although I'm hoping it's just my imagination.

'Matthew! Matthew! Matthew!' chants the crowd.

I can't believe this. No group has chanted my name since the day I won the school donut-eating competition. I downed eighteen in a minute.

'Matthew! Matthew!'

With about 20 metres to go I get a sudden spurt of energy. I run like I've never run before. It's a bit stupid when you think about it, as I've already come last.

'MATTHEW!'

But the crowd loves it.

'YAAAAAAAAAAAYYYYYYYYYY!'

Marcus Wright shakes my hand when I finish. 'Game, set and match.'

Mr Simpson calls us over. 'Class, I think we all learnt something today, about guts.'

Withers and the new kid snigger.

'I'm not talking about the guts hanging over your pants, Craig.'

The class laughs.

'I'm talking about the guts needed to do something very difficult.' Mr Simpson gestures to me to come out the front, and he shakes my hand. 'Congratulations, Matthew.'

The class clap and cheer and though I feel like spewing, I've never felt better in my life.

Chapter Nine

SPECIALS

Monday - Fried Rice	$3.00
Tuesday - Fried Lice	
(collected fresh each day)	$3.00
Wednesday - Fried Mice	$3.00
(collected fresh each night)	
Thursday - Fried Chicken Drumsticks	$3.00
(free grease)	
Friday - Fried Day	$3.00

At the start of lunch I remember that Kayla wants to talk to me, and I know exactly where to find her. I sneak up to the tuckshop line and poke her in the back.

She turns and smiles, then looks down. 'Matt, there's something I want to ask you ...'

Butterflies start flying around my gut again. My gut has actually got a bit smaller in the last week, but it can still fit a lot of butterflies.

'You know how you've been winning chocolate milks for people, like Marcus, Jasmine, Eric and Mrs Spencer?' she says.

'And you.'

She shakes her head. 'No, that was an accident. I offered to put your rubbish in the bin and it just *happened* to win.'

I raise an eyebrow. 'Whatever.'

'Well, anyway, I want to make you a deal.'

Here we go. I wonder how much it's going to cost me this time.

'If you can win me a chocolate milk today, I'll let you ask me a question. And there's a very good chance that I'll say yes.'

I wonder what the heck she's talking about. A free chocolate milk for the right to ask a question? Big woop!

Then it hits me. Surely she doesn't mean . . .

'Anything?' I ask.

'Anything. Well, almost anything.'

She looks into my eyes and the butterflies fly faster

and harder, crashing against the walls of my stomach like they're trying to perform a jailbreak. When I was at the shopping centre yesterday, I noticed a movie that I'd like to see. It doesn't even have heaps of killing in it, so Kayla might like it as well. But is this what she means?

I shake her hand. 'You've got a deal.' There's only one way to find out.

She hands me money and says to order her the special while she finds us a table.

Finds us a table?

The butterflies start coming up my throat.

Jan's away, so there's only one line leading to Mrs Dwyer. When I finally make it to the front, I order a chicken and salad sandwich, a banana, a chocolate milk, and the special – which is deep-fried chicken drumsticks.

Mrs Dwyer gives me a scowl. 'Do you really need so much food, Matthew? It's not good for you.'

'It's not all for me.'

She makes a 'humph' sound like she doesn't believe me. I can't really blame her – I used to eat this much all the time. And then she says something strange. 'Seeing Jan's not here, don't expect any boosts to your self-esteem.'

I have no idea what she means, but I don't bother asking for an explanation. I'm in a hurry to take lunch back to Kayla's and my table. Kayla's and my table. I reckon I could get used to saying that.

My heart sinks when I see Kayla sitting next to Tasha.

I stand beside them, not knowing what to do.

Tasha gives me the evil eye. 'Get lost, fat Matt.'

'I can't. I know this school too well,' I say.

'I'm going to have lunch with my friend Matthew now,' Kayla says to Tasha. 'Okay?'

It takes Tasha a few seconds to realise she's not invited, and when the penny drops so does her bottom lip. She rolls her eyes and walks off.

Kayla and I eat slowly and talk fast, which may seem normal to most kids, but to me it's not. Even though I've had some damn fine lunches, it's always been all about the food. This is different. Kayla tells me about her annoying little brother who amputated one of her Barbie doll's arms, and I tell Kayla about my mum's fruit cake that even a bird wouldn't eat. We laugh together.

'Do you feel bad about getting diabetes?' she asks.

Marcus walks past and gives me a friendly slap on the shoulder. As I nod to him, I notice boys pushing and shoving each other in the handball line.

I look back at Kayla. 'I think it's the best thing that's ever happened to me.'

I hand her the chocolate milk but she slides it back.

'I'll drink the free one,' she says. 'That's the deal.'

'I don't need it.'

'Share?'

'Okay.'

As we get close to finishing, I realise how much my life has changed in a week. Even though she can't cook

much, I now have a semi-normal mum, I can run three laps of the oval without passing out, and I'm having lunch with a girl. I'm starting to think that maybe, just maybe, I deserve all this.

I take the last gulp and get ready for greatness. But when I look at the bottom I don't see anything. I look again. There's nothing but a white piece of cardboard and tiny bits of milk in the corners, ready to be spilt.

Kayla laughs and grabs the carton, but I don't wait for her to find out that I'm a loser. As quick as a fat kid can, I get up and walk away.

Chapter Ten

SNACKS

Chips — salt and vinegar, barbeque, wood	$1.20
Jelly Cups	$0.80
Fruit Cups	$0.80
Butter Cups	$0.80
Cheese Sticks	$0.50
Liquorice Sticks	$0.15
Pogo Sticks	$80.00
Le Snack (French)	$0.75
El Snacko (Spanish)	$0.75
The Snack (English)	$0.75
Abitetoeatmate (Aussie)	$0.75
Nutella	$0.60
Utella	$0.60
Itella	$0.60
Webothtella	$0.60

I sit under a tree and think. Actually I say to myself *Why me?* over and over again. When I get sick of that I try to figure out what went wrong. I win six chocolate milks in a row. Six. And then the one time I actually need to win, the one time I get close to having something really good happen to me, I lose. Mum always says that everything happens for a reason, that it's fate. All I can say is, if fate walked up to me right now, I'd kick her in the shin.

Even the tuckshop lady was mean to me. 'Seeing Jan's not here, don't expect any boosts to your self-esteem,' Mrs Dwyer said. What the heck is that supposed to mean?

Suddenly, it hits me like a backhander. When I bought chocolate milks from Jan, I won. She's away and I lose. Perhaps it wasn't fate that let me win, but Jan? Perhaps she somehow knows which milk cartons are winners and gives them to me? But why?

Don't expect any boosts to your self-esteem. That phrase goes round and round in my head like a kebab. It occurs to me that Jan must have done it to make me feel better, 'cause I'm flabby and have no friends. Even Jan the tuckshop lady feels sorry for me, her best customer.

A wave of anger flashes through my giant gut. I hate Jan and Kayla. At least Mrs Dwyer, Withers and the new kid are honest; Jan and Kayla pretend to care but really they look down on me like everyone else. They just act nice to make themselves feel better.

'Hey, marathon man?'

It's the new kid and Withers. I really don't need this right now.

'Keep training and you might make it to the Olympics,' says the new kid. 'I heard they're bringing in a new sport called downhill rolling.'

I don't bother answering. It's not worth it. Though if they came within grabbing distance I'd crush them into human dust.

'What's wrong?' says the new kid. 'Have you eaten your own tongue?'

I look at Withers. He hasn't laughed or said anything yet, which isn't like the new him.

'Go on,' says the new kid, 'do it.' He's looking at Withers too.

Withers just stands there.

'He deserves it,' says the new kid. 'Remember what he did to you?'

Withers takes a quick step forward and throws. He doesn't chuck it full pelt – in our younger days Craig and I used to hurl rocks at plovers and I know how hard he can let one go – but nevertheless the stone stings when it smacks my leg.

I don't yelp or react, though. There's no point. I just say quietly to Withers, 'We used to be mates. Remember?'

He doesn't answer.

'Who'd want to be friends with you?' says the new kid.

They walk off.

A red mark grows on my leg, like I'm being dabbed by an invisible painter. But as it swells, the anger that I had a minute ago begins to fade, until I realise that I don't hate Kayla and Jan after all. I don't even hate Withers; I understand him too well.

Lunch is nearly over so I have to hurry. Apologising is never easy, but it's my only option. Trying to explain why I walked off will be trickier, but I'm hoping to think of something.

I turn a corner and see her back. Of all people, she's talking to Tasha, who's munching on a liquorice stick. *Great*, I think. Still, there's no time to lose.

'I hate him!' Kayla says.

I stop. Kayla hasn't seen me, though I think Tasha has. She has a nasty little smirk on her face.

'He's so pathetic it makes me sick,' Kayla continues.

Tasha looks over Kayla's shoulder at me and nods, smirking even more. Her lips are stained black from the liquorice; she looks like a devil worshipper.

'He's an ugly blob,' Kayla says, her words hitting me where it hurts.

Once again I walk away from Kayla, and this time I'm not coming back. Not this lunchtime, not ever.

Chapter Eleven

PIZZA MENU

Ham and Pineapple	$6.95
Pineapple and Ham	$6.95
Hawaiian	$6.95
Supreme	$6.95
Ultimate	$6.95
Beesknees	$6.95
Pepperoni	$6.95
Saltaroni	$6.95
Meatlovers	$6.95
Vegetablelovers	$6.95
Piecelovers	1960s
Garlic Bread	$6.95
Garlic Breath	free
Tip expected by sweaty pizza man with pimples and garlic breath	$5.00

Mum's not home after school. *Good*, I think. It gives me a chance to search the hallway cupboards and I discover a large packet of salt and vinegar chips and a bottle of coke, left over from some old party. It's like finding a hidden treasure.

Having been a health nut for a week, I full-on appreciate the first few mouthfuls of junk food. Salt, oil, sugar and fizz all burst through grateful tastebuds into my grateful belly. *Mmmmmm*, I think as I turn on the telly. Before long, though, my hand makes the journey from lap to mouth with the rest of me hardly noticing. And before long, without me hardly noticing, the food and drink are all gone.

The phone rings. 'Matthew, it's Mum.'

As if I didn't know.

'Listen, things have gone pear-shaped. The whiz-kid's messed up and clients are threatening to leave and take their money with them. Lincoln's having a cow. I'm going to have to stay until it's sorted.'

'Okay,' I say. *Typical.*

'There's some money in the bottom drawer in the kitchen. Order yourself a meal from the phone book. Something healthy, okay?'

'Okay.' *No way.*

I ring for takeaway early. Why wait? Thirty minutes later it arrives, smelling awesome.

'Large meatlovers with barbeque sauce, garlic bread and a coke,' says the pizza boy, leaning left so he can look

past me into the house. He's probably searching for my non-existent, skinny, pretty older sister.

I give him the exact money. As he passes over the pizza, I notice his shirt is soaked under the armpits. If he asks for a tip, I'll tell him to wear deodorant.

After dinner has disappeared into my stomach, I unpack the freezer. There's frozen spinach, frozen fish fingers and frozen peas. *Yuck!* But at the very back, behind some frozen water, is what I'm looking for. A full tub of chocolate ice-cream.

I don't think I have much at all, but when Mum unlocks the front door and I wake up – on the couch – I look down and notice it's nearly all gone.

Mum sees the pizza box and the ice-cream tub and I can tell she's not happy, but all she says is 'Clean your teeth and go to bed'. By the time I come out of the bathroom she's already plugged in her laptop and opened a bottle of wine.

Old habits die hard.

Chapter Twelve

KISSING MENU

Lip Peck	$1.00
Cheek Peck	$0.50
Chicken Peck	$0.50
French (free tongue)	$2.00
Russian (served quickly)	$1.50
Hairy Uncle	$0.20
Hairy Aunty	$0.20
Soft Lips	$1.20
Chapped Lips	$0.80
Dead Fish	$0.60

As I line up for tuckshop, two things make me happy:

1. *Jan's back.*

2. *It's Friday, which means fresh meat pies.*

Someone pokes me from behind. I don't turn around. The poking gets harder. Still I ignore it.

Now it's two-finger poking, like someone is typing a book on my back. I spin 180 degrees, angry.

Before I can say anything someone grabs my shoulders and my lips are smacked by . . . lips! It takes a second for me to realise it's Kayla, and that she's planted a kiss right on my kisser!

I'm too shocked to react. She pulls me out of line, and a boy who saw what happened gives me the thumbs-up. We sit at the same table as yesterday, but I'm having trouble thinking straight. I can feel someone else's spit on my top lip.

'Why'd you do that for?' I ask.

'I don't know,' Kayla says. She looks shocked too. 'Felt like it, I s'pose.'

'Couldn't you, like, have asked me first?'

'Yeah, I should've. Sorry.'

'I think it's illegal what you did. It's, like, lip abuse.'

'I said I was sorry.' She looks down. 'So you didn't like it?'

I'm not sure what to say, so I lick my top lip. It tastes like girl.

'Why'd you leave yesterday?' she asks, still staring at the ground.

'Because . . .'

'Because why?'

'I didn't win.'

She looks back up. 'You think I care about a free chocolate milk?'

I think for a second. 'Yes.'

She smiles. 'You're right, I do. But I care about you more.'

Hearing that makes me tingle all over, like when I drink frozen coke too fast. Then I remember what she said about me. 'You called me ugly and pathetic.'

'Excuse me?'

'Yesterday. I heard you.'

'When?'

'At the end of lunch. You were talking to Tasha. I came back to apologise and I heard what you said.'

She's quiet for a second, thinking. Then she remembers and her mouth opens. 'I was talking about Craig Withers. Tasha told me he threw a rock at you.'

My mouth opens too. 'Really?'

'Really.'

This is getting mega weird. I suppose it's possible she's telling the truth. But there's one more thing I need to know.

'Why would you even like me?' I ask. 'Especially when I'm . . .'

'Fat?'

'Yeah.'

'I don't care about that.'

It's hard for me to believe. 'Why not?'

She takes out her wallet, and for a second I think she's going to pay me back all the money I've lent her this year. Instead, she takes out a family photo. Her mum and her brother look normal, but her dad's big smile appears out of butt-sized cheeks, and his tummy looks like it has swallowed a small car.

'That's one big bloke,' I say.

'That's my dad.' She looks at the photo and speaks to it, quietly. 'I love him.'

I get up and Kayla grabs my arm. 'You're not leaving again, are you?'

'There's something I have to do.'

By this time the tuckshop line is not long.

'Young Matthew, so nice to see you,' Jan says.

'How are you feeling today?' I ask.

'Much better. I think it was just one of those 24-hour things. How are you going?'

'Good. But I'd be even better if I could have a chocolate milk.' I lean in closer. 'A lucky one, if possible.'

There's a twinkle in her eye. 'You've had a lot of luck lately.'

'I know. But if I could have just a little bit more, I think my life will be perfect.'

When I return, placing the chocolate milk in front of her, Kayla gives me a questioning look.

'Drink it,' I say. 'If it says "Winner" at the bottom I'll let you ask me a question.'

'Anything?' she says.

'Anything.' Then I hold up my hand. 'Well, *almost* anything.'

We smile together.

Chapter Thirteen

MOVIE MENU

Maltesers	$3.90
Miketeasers	$3.90
Fantales	$3.60
More Fantales (I kissed a pop star)	$3.80
Fairytales (I married a pop star and lived happily ever after)	$3.80
Kit Kat	$2.90
Hit Cat	$2.90
Dead Cat	9 lives all up
Soft drink – Maxi	$4.80
Soft drink – Mega	$4.79
Soft drink – Super	$4.78
Soft drink – Notsmallbecausecustomerswon'tbuysmall	$4.77

Later that day I'm called to the office. I'm surprised to see Mum waiting. 'Doctor's appointment,' she says.

I forgot about it.

Mum and I don't talk in the car; we just listen to music. As she pulls into the carpark her mobile rings, but for the first time ever she doesn't answer it. She turns to me instead. 'Let's be honest in there, okay?'

I nod.

She looks in the rear-view mirror and smooths down her hair. There's still a bare patch, but it's not quite as big as it was. Mum has been letting the new hair grow.

'So how'd the first week of the rest of your life go, Matthew?' Doctor Morrison asks.

'Pretty good. Just one slip-up. A big one.'

He looks serious. 'Mmm, I see.' He turns to my mum. 'And how about your week, Lorraine?'

'One slip-up as well.' She looks at me. 'Change is hard.'

'You're dead right,' Doctor Morrison says.

I hate it when a doctor uses the D word.

I get weighed and doc's happy because I've lost a kilogram, though I reckon it'd be at least two if it hadn't been for last night.

We sit down again. 'Good news, Matthew. While the tests last week indicate impaired glucose tolerance, it looks like a fully blown case of type 2 diabetes hasn't yet developed.'

'Huh?' I say.

'You don't have diabetes. Though if you're not careful you'll get it.'

I sigh with relief. So does Mum.

We're all quiet for a few seconds.

'Do you know what a cycle is, Matthew?' the doc asks.

'Something you ride to the park?'

He smiles. 'True. It's also a way of explaining why things happen. When you eat well and exercise you feel better, which makes you want to keep eating well and exercising even more. That's what's called a positive cycle.'

I notice the jellybeans on his desk. Though I don't have to have one, I wouldn't say no if he offered.

He continues: 'When you eat poorly you don't have much energy, so you don't want to exercise. And when people tease you about being overweight you feel bad about yourself, so you eat more. That's a negative cycle.'

I'd probably choose red if I could, followed by yellow, then green.

'By the sounds of it you're starting to get into a positive cycle, but it's easy to slip back because it's what you're used to. You're lucky 'cause you have your mum to help you. How about friends?'

Mum gives a quick shake of the head, trying to tell the doctor that I don't have any.

But I do. 'I've got a girlfriend,' I say. 'She's real nice. We're seeing a movie tonight. Well, if it's all right with you, Mum?'

Mum looks shocked.

'That's great,' Doctor Morrison says. 'Give people a chance to like you. I'm sure lots of them will. But if some people are mean to you, it's their problem, not yours. Okay?'

He shakes my hand.

Damn! No jellybeans.

While waiting to buy movie tickets I get punched in the gut. Not from Kayla – she's gone to buy us a Slush Puppy to share (the doc said it was better than popcorn) – but from Eric.

'Do you know that guy over there?' he asks, pointing.

I can't answer. I'm still winded.

'It's my brother,' Eric continues. 'He delivers pizza.'

I look closer now, and come to think of it the guy does seem familiar. I recognise his sweaty armpits.

'Pizza isn't fried,' I say. 'It's baked.'

He punches me again. 'I don't care.'

He walks away, stops, and then turns. I get ready to run. 'You know, you and Kayla look good together,' he says. 'Enjoy the movie.'

I'm too nervous to enjoy anything, but it's a good kind of nervous. It makes me hungry.

Not for food, though.

For life.